nickelodeon™

DoRa & DieGo

DORA AND DIEGO HELP THE LITTLE WOLF

adapted by Christine Ricci
based on the screenplay "Little Lost Wolf Pup"
written by Valerie Walsh

illustrated by Art Mawhinney

Turn the page to learn with me and my very best buddy, Zee!

Based on the TV series *Go, Diego, Go!*™ as seen on Nick Jr.™
This book was previously published as *Diego's Wolf Pup Rescue*.

SIMON SPOTLIGHT/NICKELODEON
An imprint of Simon & Schuster Children's Publishing Division
New York London Toronto Sydney
1230 Avenue of the Americas, New York, New York 10020

For information about special discounts for bulk purchases, please contact Simon & Schuster Special Sales at 1-866-506-1949 or business@simonandschuster.com.
Manufactured in the United States of America 0911 LAK This Simon Spotlight edition 2011 2 4 6 8 10 9 7 5 3 1 ISBN 978-1-4424-2863-8

In this book, you will learn to . . .

✓  **READ** with us

 MOVE with us

 SHARE and CARE with us

 DISCOVER with us

 CREATE with us

 EXPLORE with us

✓ **COUNT** with us

 **MAKE MUSIC** with us

Hey there! I'm Moose and this is Zee. We're so glad you picked up this book today. We can't wait for you to find out what happens in this story!

Dora and Diego are on the way
to rescue a wolf pup and save the day.
Mami Wolf wants her pup to come home—
that lost little wolf pup is all alone!
To rescue him, Dora and Diego need
help from YOU! So come on! Let's read!

 Check out the last page for a play-along counting activity!

"We're Animal Rescuers!" shouted Diego as he slid down the pole from the Animal Rescue Center's observation platform.

"Animal Rescuers!" chanted his cousin Dora as she followed Diego down the pole.

Dora was visiting the Animal Rescue Center, and Diego had a special surprise for her.

"Watch this!" said Diego as he cupped his hand to his mouth and called, "Ah-ruff! Ah-ruff!"

Suddenly several maned wolf pups poked their heads out of the tall grass. *"Ah-ruff! Ah-ruff!"* they barked.

"Maned wolf pups!" said Dora excitedly. "What a great surprise!"

The pups playfully scampered over to Diego and Dora.
"They're so small!" giggled Dora as the pups climbed on her.
"And this one is the littlest," said Diego as he stroked the tiny pup's fur.

Just then Diego's sister Alicia arrived with Mommy Maned Wolf. "Mommy Maned Wolf came to the Rescue Center to have her wolf pups," Alicia explained.

Dora turned to Mommy Maned Wolf. "Your little pups are so cute. And there are so many of them!"

"Maned wolves can have up to five pups at a time," Mommy Maned Wolf said proudly.

"How many pups are there?" asked Diego. "Let's count them."

Dora and Diego counted the wolf pups: one, two, three, four. Four maned wolf pups!

Mommy Maned Wolf gasped. "Only *four* maned wolf pups?" she asked. "But I have *five* pups! My littlest pup is missing!"

"Don't worry, Mommy Maned Wolf!" said Diego. "We're Animal Rescuers. We'll find your littlest pup."

Alicia decided to stay at the Animal Rescue Center to help Mommy Maned Wolf with the other pups. "Go, Animal Rescuers! Go!" she cheered as Diego and Dora ran off toward the Science Deck.

Diego and Dora ran over to their special camera, Click.
"Click can help us find the baby maned wolf," said Diego.

Click zoomed through the forest and found the little wolf pup.

"He's heading for the prickers and thorns!" said Diego, watching closely. "He could get hurt."

"We've got to rescue him!" said Dora.

"*¡Al rescate!*" shouted Diego. "To the rescue!"

Diego and Dora jumped on a zip cord and zoomed through the forest. They landed at a fork in the road. "Look!" said Diego. "There are prints on each path."

"But which ones belong to the baby maned wolf?" Dora asked.

Diego pulled out his Field Journal and scrolled to a picture of a maned wolf's paw print. "Which path has prints that look like these?" he asked.

"These prints match," exclaimed Dora as she pointed to the third path. "¡Vámonos! Let's go!"

The path led them to a river. Diego pulled out his spotting scope and located the wolf pup's prints on the far bank. "We need to get across this river to keep following the wolf pup's tracks," said Diego.

"I can help!" called out Rescue Pack.

"Me too!" chimed in Backpack.

Rescue Pack and Backpack worked together to help get Diego and Dora across the river. Rescue Pack transformed himself into a raft. Backpack gave them paddles and a life jacket.

After turning his vest into a second life jacket, Diego jumped into the raft next to Dora. They started to paddle down the river. Suddenly Diego noticed a river otter stuck in a whirlpool. "We have to rescue the river otter!" he shouted.

Diego threw a life preserver to the river otter, and the river otter scrambled onto it. Then Diego and Dora pulled the river otter to safety.

"Thanks for rescuing me," said the river otter.

"We're Animal Rescuers," replied Diego. "It's what we do!"

Once on shore Diego and Dora ran toward the prickers and thorns. But when they arrived, the little maned wolf was nowhere in sight. Diego cupped his hands to his ears to listen for the pup. Finally he heard a bark.

"Ah-ruff!"

"It sounds like he's in these bushes," said Diego.

Diego and Dora stretched up tall to see over the pricker and thorn bushes.

The little maned wolf was heading toward a sharp prickly bush!
"Stop, Baby Maned Wolf!" called Diego and Dora. "Stop!"
Baby Maned Wolf heard the warning and stopped right in front of the
sharp prickly bush.

Diego and Dora ran over to the little wolf pup and knelt down next to him.

"Hi, Baby Maned Wolf!" Diego said. "We're Animal Rescuers! You're safe now!"

"Thanks for rescuing me," said Baby Maned Wolf. "I can't wait to see my mommy and my brothers and sisters."

Back at the Animal Rescue Center, Mommy Maned Wolf nuzzled her littlest pup and made sure he wasn't hurt. Baby Maned Wolf was so happy to be with his family that he jumped into Diego's arms and gave him a big lick on the cheek.

Then Baby Maned Wolf curled up next to the other pups and fell fast asleep.

"*¡Misión cumplida!* Rescue complete!" whispered Diego. "That was a great animal adventure!"

Dear parents,

We hope your child enjoyed this exciting Dora and Diego adventure. To extend the story, have a conversation with your child about it. You could ask what his favorite part was and why. Or have him tell you about a time he helped a friend in need, just like Dora and Diego.

This book is also a great starting point for talking to your child about the importance of math and counting. Remind him that Dora and Diego's counting helped them discover that one of the wolf pups was missing. Math and counting are used in everyday ways, too. Here's a counting game your child will enjoy playing with you, using objects around your home:

Let's Go on a Shopping Adventure!

From your friends at Nickelodeon and Simon Spotlight

Tell your child you are going to pretend the two of you are at the store. Your child is the salesperson and you will tell him what things you need.

Then name items for your child to collect around your home, giving a specific number each time. ("I need three pencils, five crayons, and two apples.")

Have your child collect the objects and count them as he gives them to you.

You can alternate between being the shopper and the salesperson, and have your child tell you which items to collect. Your child will love showing you how well he can count!

Now, let's get counting!